GOLD Fever

Dear Reader

At some time or another, everyone dreams about becoming wealthy. Imagine how fantastic it would feel if you were lucky enough to discover a giant nugget of precious gold, for example!

MORE OFTEN THAN NOT, THEIR DREAMS OF WEALTH CAME TO NOTHING.

Throughout history, the same dream has inspired countless thousands of people to seek their fortunes in gold rushes around the world. A few lucky gold prospectors did find giant nuggets of precious gold. But more often than not, people's dreams of wealth came to nothing. The legacy that they left behind, however, has changed countries, cultures and societies.

I hope you enjoy this book – and, who knows? Maybe by reading it, you might catch gold fever, too!

John Parsons

NELSON
CENGAGE Learning™
For learning solutions, visit cengage.com.au

Contents

GOLD Fever

MT ALEXANDER GOLD DIGGINGS from Adelaide Hill

1 What Causes Gold Fever?

The Thrill of Discovery

Imagine a cube that is around 20 metres wide, deep and tall. Now, imagine it filled with gold. That cube would weigh around 165 000 tonnes and be worth over five trillion dollars. Over the entire period of human history, that cube would represent nearly all the gold that humans have ever mined and collected. It would also represent the thrill and excitement of the countless thousands of people who discovered every tiny speck, grain and nugget of gold in that cube.

20 metres

20 metres

20 metres

$5 000 000 000 000!

Gold is the only yellow metal found on Earth. It is mostly found in the form of nuggets, or in quartz as grains. Gold is one of the softest, densest metals that exist. For this reason, it can be moulded easily into different shapes.

Its softness also enables it to be mixed with other metals to make it stronger. Gold does not rust and lasts a long time.

Although gold can be found in most countries, it is rare. For this reason, it is treated as extremely precious and desirable by most people.

Gold has been used for many things, including money, jewellery, medicine and – most of all – to demonstrate the wealth and the power of those people who can afford to own it.

Golden masks such as that of Tutankhamun (left) demonstrated the power and wealth of the Egyptian pharaohs. Massive golden statues of Buddha (right) show how much people respect and revere their religious leaders.

AZTEC GOLD

The Aztec civilisation, which thrived between 1300–1500 in central Mexico, North America, used gold for decoration – but cacao beans and cotton cloth had more value and were used for money. The Spanish, believing the Aztecs had huge stores of gold, defeated the Aztecs in 1521, and destroyed their civilisation.

This painting of Popocatepetl (left) and Iztaccihuatl, an Aztec prince and princess, shows them wearing ceremonial gold to demonstrate their status.

For every gold miner who strikes it lucky, there may be a thousand who end up with nothing. The great outbreaks of gold fever in Australia, New Zealand and the USA made a few people extremely wealthy and left tens of thousands disappointed – but they also resulted in the growth of those developing countries. Gold fever has left a legacy that we can still see today, in the buildings and the diverse cultures that call these areas home.

For a long time, gold has been of huge economic, cultural, social and political significance around the world. Many people's lives have been affected by gold. As it becomes increasingly rare, it will continue to influence people's lives.

Maybe so, Mr Shakespeare, but this sure looks attractive to me!

A FAMOUS SAYING

"All that glitters is not gold."

This saying from William Shakespeare (1564–1616) is still used today. It means that not everything that looks attractive has real value.

2 A Rare and Precious Metal

What Is Gold?

Gold is a chemical element that occurs as a metal, like iron, copper and lead. But its rarity, compared to other metals, has meant that people have always considered it more valuable.

The arrangement of the atoms inside gold means that, unlike most other metals, which are grey or silvery, it reflects yellow light. This "golden" colouring makes it attractive for jewellery and decoration.

SYMBOL FOR GOLD

The chemical symbol for gold is "Au", which comes from *aurum*, the Latin word for gold.

ALCHEMY

Alchemy was a process by which people hoped to turn cheap metals, such as lead, into valuable metals, such as gold. Until the 1600s, people thought a mythical substance called the "philosopher's stone" could help them do this. Although alchemy never worked, it did help people start to understand chemistry, which became a proper science towards the end of the 1600s.

WORTH ITS WEIGHT IN GOLD!

Because of its chemical and physical structure, gold does not react easily with many other chemicals. It does not rust when it is exposed to air and water, and it does not corrode when it comes into contact with many acids. It is also very heavy. A cubic metre of aluminium weighs 2.7 tonnes. The same volume of gold weighs 19.3 tonnes.

NUGGETS AND GRAINS

As it does not react with other chemicals, gold is almost always found naturally as a metal – either as large lumps, called nuggets, or as grains inside other rocks. The largest gold nugget ever found was discovered in Victoria, Australia, in 1869. It weighed an incredible 78 kilograms, which at today's value would be worth about $A 1.8 million. Two miners, John Deason and Richard Oates, found the nugget, which they named the "Welcome Stranger", lying less than 10 centimetres underground, near the roots of a tree.

a replica of the "Welcome Stranger" (above) and the monument marking its place of discovery at Moliagul, Victoria (right)

gold is used in satellites (left) and, from top to bottom below, in gold sheets, gold wire, to colour glass, to decorate food, in electronics and in dentistry

In addition to being valuable and attractive for making jewellery and other decorations, the properties of gold make it a useful metal in other areas.

Gold is extremely malleable, which means it can be easily pressed or flattened into different shapes. One gram of gold can be flattened into a sheet one square metre in size, so thin that light can shine through it. It is also the most ductile metal known, which means it can be pulled or stretched into long wires. Gold is an excellent conductor of electricity, and is also used to colour glass red, to repel radiation on satellites, as a luxury food decoration, as a filling for teeth and for many other applications.

The McLaren F1 supercar, which is the world's fastest road car, even uses gold foil in its engine compartment. The gold foil, in combination with the car's speed and rarity, may be why one McLaren F1 sold for $4 million in 2008!

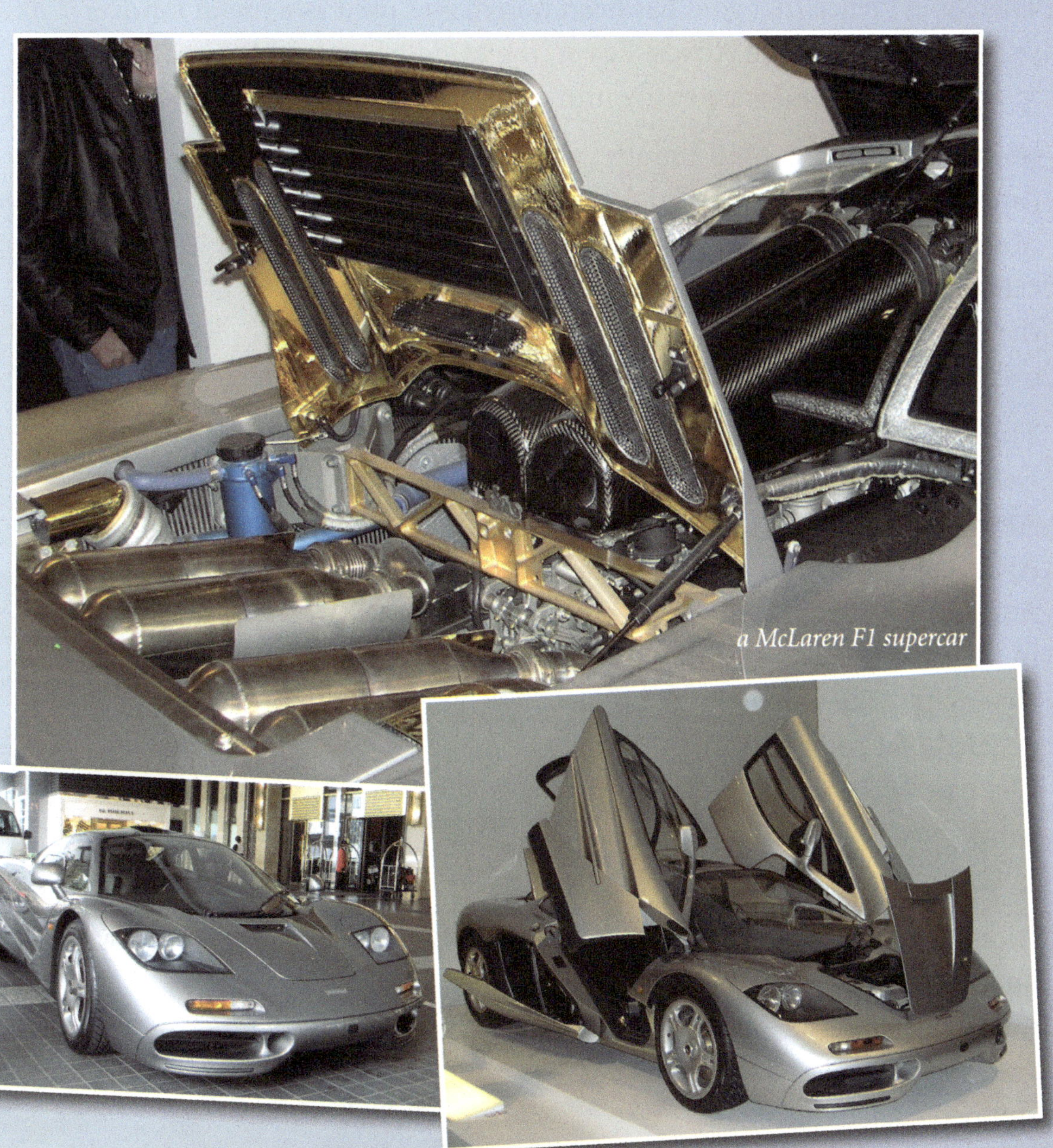
a McLaren F1 supercar

3 The Age of the Gold Rush

Get Rich Quick!

There is evidence that gold has been mined and used as a metal for over 7000 years. Certain areas in Africa, Egypt, the Middle East and Europe were rich in gold deposits and were easily mined.

In the West African Mali Empire, which existed in medieval times, gold was very plentiful. When its emperor, Mansa Musa, visited Egypt in the fourteenth century, he gave away so much gold that the Egyptians complained that their own gold had become worthless.

The first Spanish explorers who went to Central and South America found that Native Americans, such as the Aztecs, used lots of gold in their jewellery and ornaments. They soon decided that colonising that part of the world would be a good way to get rich quick.

If this golden Aztec shield featuring the Aztec god Tonahtiuh had been found by the Spanish, they would have seized it and melted it down.

Along with silver and precious gems, enormous amounts of gold were seized and shipped back to Spain.

Later, as new European colonies sprang up in North America, Australia and New Zealand, gold was discovered in these regions, too. For the impoverished settlers, labourers and farm workers who had emigrated to these countries, it suddenly became possible to become instantly rich beyond their wildest dreams.

Wherever gold was found, there was an immediate rush of newcomers, desperate to seek their fortune. Each miner wanted to be among the first to get as much gold as they could. Every miner wanted to find the next "Welcome Stranger". Gold rushes occurred throughout the nineteenth century. Although every miner dreamed of becoming wealthy, it was usually the people who set up shops, services, and buildings who ended up rich.

GOLD FEVER HITS BRAZIL

One of the first recorded gold rushes happened in Brazil, South America, in the 1690s. Portuguese slave hunters, called *bandeirantes*, who had ventured into the rainforest of Brazil in search of Native Americans, found gold instead. Within a few years, more than 400 000 Portuguese rushed to Brazil, hoping to get rich. They forced about half a million African slaves to come with them and work in the rainforest. Much of the gold that was extracted from the rainforest helped make Portugal a wealthy colonial power. The people who stayed helped to make Brazil a colourful mix of cultures and identities – and their descendents still speak mostly Portuguese.

GARIMPEIROS

Brazil still has about 400 000 gold prospectors or *garimpeiros*. Each year, Brazil produces over 50 tonnes of gold, much of it found by *garimpeiros* using old-fashioned methods, such as gold panning.

See map on page 25!

GOLD FEVER HITS CALIFORNIA

When gold was discovered in North America in California, in 1848, it started a huge gold rush. Over 300 000 people raced to California from the rest of the USA, as well as from Latin America and Europe. By 1852, 20 000 people were arriving each year from China.

Posters and advertisements like the one above enticed gold miners to San Francisco.

San Francisco, which had been a small, quiet settlement, turned into a booming city that serviced the needs of the huge influx of people. In two years, the city's population exploded from 1 000 to 25 000 people.

The painting above shows gold miners working and trading with Native Americans in California.

In 1848, California wasn't officially a state of the USA and it had few laws. Greedy gold miners forced Native Americans off their lands, and it is estimated that over 100 000 Native Americans died as a result of the violence, disease and land confiscations that the gold rush brought.

This early photo shows the rough, crowded conditions in which gold miners lived and worked.

Crime and violence between different ethnic groups on the goldfields also contributed to California's reputation as a lawless territory.

In 1850, the USA, realising how important this area had suddenly become, made California a state.

See map on page 25!

GOLD FEVER HITS AUSTRALIA

Gold was discovered in many regions of Australia in the nineteenth century. But the biggest gold rush occurred in the state of Victoria in the 1850s and 1860s. The discovery of vast amounts of gold caused the Australian population to triple during those decades.

Thousands of miners streamed into the towns of Ballarat, Bendigo and Beechworth. They found so much gold that, at the height of the gold rush, two tonnes of gold every week was taken into Melbourne's Treasury Building.

The discovery of gold in Australia had far-reaching consequences for the country's social development. There were many tensions around land ownership and the rights and conditions of workers in the mines. Gold also saw the influx of many different ethnic groups. The way in which they, and the original inhabitants of Australia, were treated, led to many discussions around what sort of society Australia should become.

See map on page 25!

Discontent around the laws and the conditions under which they were forced to work led to a number of uprisings, including the Eureka rebellion in 1854. This led to a more democratic approach and a fairer system of laws and rules that changed the way Australia was governed.

THE EUREKA REBELLION

Unhappy with taxes, expensive mining licenses and official interference, gold miners in Ballarat, Victoria, decided to protest. On 3 December 1854, the miners and government soldiers fought a battle at Eureka Stockade. Over 30 people died, but the miners eventually won the right to vote and buy land, which was an important step towards democracy in Australia.

The Eureka flag (above) was first used by the miners at Eureka Stockade.

This painting from the 1850s shows gold miners camping and working near Bendigo, Victoria.

Bendigo – A Golden Legacy

The city of Bendigo is a major regional centre in Victoria, Australia. It is about 150 kilometres north of the capital, Melbourne, and has about 90 000 residents. It is over 160 years old and is named after the Bendigo Creek that runs through its centre. Bendigo is at the heart of the area where gold was discovered in 1851, and its people, architecture and history reflect the influence of the gold boom that it underwent in the second half of the nineteenth century.

Bendigo's original inhabitants were the Dja Dja Wrung people, who lived in the area between the Loddon and Avoca rivers. There is evidence that as early as 1789, the Dja Dja Wrung people suffered from smallpox, a deadly disease brought by European settlers, but there is no record of how this came to be passed to the Dja Dja Wrung people.

a squatter sets up his camp in Victoria, near Bendigo

In 1836, the explorer and surveyor Thomas Mitchell (1792–1855) came to central Victoria to survey its lands.

He reported that he had found large, fertile plains. As a result, the next year, many squatters arrived to take land for sheep runs.

The middle of 1851 was an eventful time for the people of this part of the world. Victoria broke away from New South Wales and formed its own colony. Then, a few days later, the discovery of gold at Clunes, near Ballarat, marked the start of the Victorian Gold Rush.

a scene from Bendigo in 1851, showing settlers and the area's original inhabitants

Later that year, two women who lived on one of the squatter's runs, Margaret Kennedy and Julia Farrell, found gold in an area of the Bendigo Creek. Although they tried to keep their discovery secret, they were spotted with their gold by a journalist who reported what he saw to the newspapers in Melbourne. Within weeks, the rush to Bendigo started.

In 1851, the total population of Victoria was 75 000 people. Two years later, it was over 500 000.

Tens of thousands of hopeful gold miners flooded into Bendigo, living in filthy, overcrowded tent cities. As well as miners from Europe, the USA and other parts of Australia, Bendigo attracted between 3 000 and 4 000 Chinese miners from the Guangdong province in south-eastern China, who named Bendigo *Dai Gum San* (or the "Big Gold Mountain").

a Chinese miner, Bendigo

In 1855, the government of the time decided to tax Chinese miners who wanted to disembark from their ships in Melbourne. To avoid the tax, many Chinese people went to Adelaide and walked overland to Bendigo, a distance of around 600 kilometres.

Since 1851, over 700 000 kilograms of gold have been found in Bendigo. It still has working gold mines, and is the seventh largest producer of gold in the world.

Today, Bendigo is a thriving centre, where around 90 000 people live. Its colourful and wealthy past as a gold mining town can be seen in its many ornate Victorian buildings, such as the town hall, post office, law courts and opera house. The Chinese influence is also kept alive, both through the descendents of Chinese miners who decided to stay in Australia, and through its "joss house", a temple built in the 1860s by the Chinese emigrants. Bendigo's joss house is the only surviving building of its kind in regional Victoria that continues to be used as a place of worship.

central Bendigo (below) and the ornate Victorian town hall (below inset)

Bendigo's cultural heritage is also recorded and celebrated in its Golden Dragon Museum. This museum is built where the original Chinese emigrants lived and worked, and has beautiful Chinese gardens and a temple to the Buddhist goddess of mercy, Kuan Yin.

the beautiful Chinese gardens at Bendigo's Golden Dragon Museum (above left) and the ornate entrance (below left)

The Golden Dragon Museum is also home to the world's oldest and longest Chinese ceremonial dragons. Sun Loong, the longest dragon, is over 100 metres long. The oldest dragon, Loong, was in the parade to celebrate federation in 1901 and the parade to celebrate the centenary of federation in 2001.

Every Easter, Sun Loong is woken from his sleep by drummers, and is paraded through Bendigo (above); visitors to Bendigo can still experience the thrill of finding gold (right).

Visitors to Bendigo can also experience what it was like for gold miners by visiting the Central Deborah Gold Mine, which has been tunnelled more than 400 metres underground. After most of the surface gold was discovered, miners had to build mines like the Central Deborah mine to reach gold buried deep underground.

Bendigo is a very different place to the tent city it was in the 1850s, when it was home to hopeful miners from around the world. Bendigo's gold may have made some of its first inhabitants rich – but the descendents of those miners have ensured that twenty-first century Bendigo is a city rich in architectural heritage and cultural diversity.

GOLD FEVER HITS NEW ZEALAND

Gabriel Read, an Australian miner who had already been in both the Californian and Australian gold rushes, found gold in Central Otago, New Zealand, in 1861.

By the end of that year, 14 000 gold miners had rushed to the region, many of them coming from the goldfields in Victoria. Like previous gold rushes, there were also many Chinese emigrants who came to seek their fortune. Dunedin, New Zealand's most southerly city, grew quickly and soon became the country's biggest and wealthiest city. But, within a few years, less and less gold was discovered and many of the emigrants either left New Zealand or stayed to start up farms, market gardens or other endeavours.

a gold miner walks across Central Otago in search of gold (left); a group of Chinese miners from the 1860s (below left); a stagecoach carrying gold gets ready to set off for Dunedin (below right)

See map on page 25!

GOLD FEVER HITS CANADA

In the freezing Arctic conditions of northern Canada, a Native American man called Skookum Jim discovered gold in 1896. The news soon spread and the Klondike River in Yukon became the scene of a massive gold rush.

Many people in the USA were having financial difficulty at the time, and the lure of gold proved too much for many of them. Within two years, 40 000 miners had made the trip through Alaska or through Canada to the Klondike. There were so many people crowded into this harsh wilderness that starvation was a real threat to the population.

A TONNE OF FOOD!

The Canadian government passed laws insisting that every miner would have to bring at least a tonne of supplies and food into the area if they wanted to mine there. They also set up checkpoints to take away the miners' guns and weapons. It was not only crime that the government feared – they also thought that if enough gold was discovered, the Americans who had travelled to Canada might want to set up their own state!

Many women joined the Klondike gold rush, and some became successful miners.

Since 1891, over 390 000 kilograms of gold have been discovered around the Klondike area.

Wharves along the west coast of the USA were overwhelmed as people rushed to sail north.

See map on page 25!

A Changed World

Each of these gold rushes had far-reaching effects on the people, the societies and the environments of the places where they occurred. Many of the places that were born from gold fever became large, established cities, as the gold ran out and the miners and their descendents found other opportunities and lifestyles. Even today, the legacy of these gold rushes can be seen in the mixture of cultures and ethnic groups that make up these modern cities and in the grand architecture that was built with the money that came from the gold discoveries. The tensions that arose between different groups during the gold rushes have also resulted in fairer laws and a better understanding of cultural differences. Today, all these cities celebrate their colourful history and take pride in the individuals and groups who contributed to the growth of their cities and communities during that period.

a painting of gold prospectors in the Sierra mountains between California and Nevada

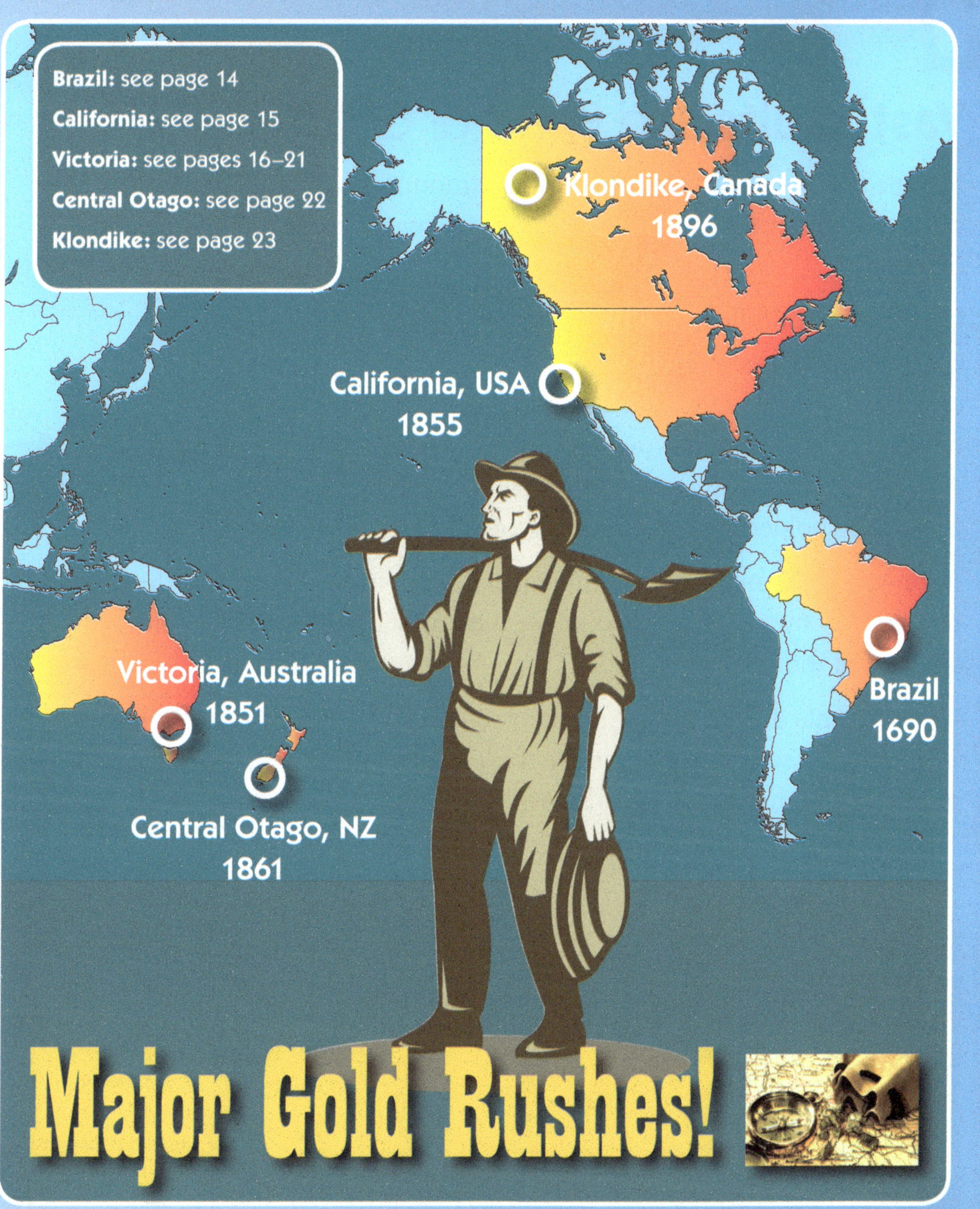

Major Gold Rushes!

4 Show Me the Money!

Vast Vaults and Bricks of Gold

No one throws away gold – so the vast amount of gold that has been discovered around the world is still being worn, used, bought and sold, or stored.

Up until the middle of the twentieth century, governments held vast stores of gold as a backstop for the money and coins that they and their people used. A banknote was really only a promise by the government to give the holder the same amount of gold if they wanted to swap it.

Because governments eventually needed more money than just the amount of gold they owned, they gradually gave up the idea of only printing that amount of money and no more.

Governments do still hold onto their reserves of gold, however, and sometimes these are traded between governments that owe each other money.

a reserve of gold (above) and the door to the vault in which it is stored (left)

AN ENORMOUS GOLD VAULT

Some governments keep their gold in special vaults in their own countries. But the biggest gold vault in the world is at 33 Liberty Street in New York, USA. There, many governments from around the world store their gold at the Federal Reserve Bank of New York building.

At 33 Liberty Street, over 7000 tonnes of gold are held in an enormous vault 25 metres below ground level. That amount of gold is worth over $300 billion.

For centuries, countries were only allowed to print as much money as they held in gold reserves. The Federal Reserve's logo still appears on US banknotes.

a rare glimpse inside the New York vault

Fort Knox, Kentucky, USA

Even though it holds less gold, the gold depository at Fort Knox in Kentucky, USA, is more well-known than the Federal Reserve Bank. Fort Knox is on the corner of Bullion Boulevard and Gold Vault Road, and over 4600 tonnes of gold are stored there. Fort Knox is heavily guarded and has many security systems, including 22-tonne doors that can only be opened by several people keying in different combinations at the same time.

It is so secure and safe that during World War II, irreplaceable items such as the US Declaration of Independence, the English Magna Carta, and the crown jewels from some European countries were kept there.

SO WHO OWNS WHAT?

Here's a list of the 40 governments that hold the most gold in the world:

Country	Tonnes of Gold
United States	8 133.5
Germany	3 401.8
Italy	2 451.8
France	2 435.4
China	1 054.1
Switzerland	1 040.1
Russia	775.2
Japan	765.2
Netherlands	612.5
India	557.7
Taiwan	423.6
Portugal	382.5
Venezuela	363.9
Saudi Arabia	322.9
United Kingdom	310.3
Lebanon	286.8
Spain	281.6
Austria	280.0
Belgium	227.5
Pakistan	184.4

Country	Tonnes of Gold
Philippines	175.9
Algeria	173.6
Libya	143.8
Singapore	127.4
Sweden	125.7
South Africa	124.9
Turkey	116.1
Greece	111.7
Romania	103.7
Poland	102.9
Thailand	99.5
Australia	79.9
Kuwait	79.0
Egypt	75.6
Indonesia	73.1
Kazakhstan	67.3
Denmark	66.5
Argentina	54.7
Finland	49.1
Bulgaria	39.9

PRIVATE GOLD

Despite the huge reserves of gold held by governments, over half of the world's gold is used and re-used for jewellery. The biggest fans of gold jewellery are by far the people of India. Every year, Indians buy about 800 tonnes of gold, or around a quarter of the new gold mined each year.

Because gold is soft compared to other metals, it is often mixed with copper or silver when it is made into jewellery. The number of carats describing a piece of jewellery shows how pure the gold in it is.

a woman from India wearing traditional gold jewellery

A 24-carat piece of jewellery is pure gold. An 18-carat piece of jewellery has 75 per cent gold and 25 per cent copper or other metals.

BUYING AND SELLING

People, as well as governments, can buy and sell gold. Many countries, such as the USA, Australia and South Africa, issue special coins made of gold that can be collected and traded by anyone who can afford them.

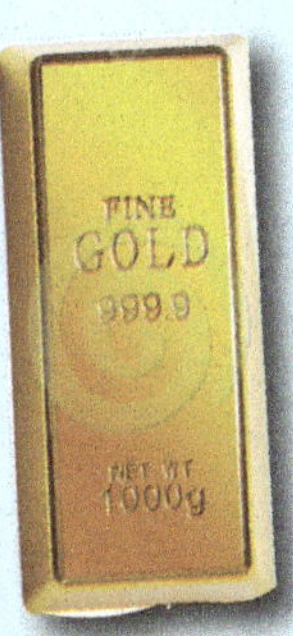

People can also buy gold bars. Instead of keeping their savings in the bank, or in other investments such as shares in companies, they may prefer to have something that they think will always be valuable. The brick-shaped gold bars we see in movies are about 12 kilograms in weight, but private traders prefer smaller, flatter bars called "kilobars". These weigh exactly one kilogram. The largest gold bar was made in Japan in 2005 and weighed 250 kilograms.

5 The Thrill of Discovery

People Love to Find Gold

Even though there are no longer gold rushes and gold may be bought and sold by people who have enough money to do so, there is one thing that has not changed: gold fever.

The excitement that people feel when they discover gold is still a thrill. Luckily, we don't have to endure hard work in terrible conditions to experience it. Many of the towns and cities that were built upon the original gold fever during the gold rushes know that people love to find gold – and they've turned it into a tourist activity.

At gold museums and theme parks, such as Ballarat's Sovereign Hill in Australia, kids and adults can experience a taste of gold fever for themselves. And, just as it was with the gold rushes 150 years ago, whatever you find is yours to keep.

Good luck – and remember: just because the "Welcome Stranger" was the biggest gold nugget discovered so far, it doesn't mean there's not another one even bigger, sitting a few centimetres under the ground somewhere. All you have to do is go and find it.

Welcome to gold fever!

Index

Glossary

chemistry A branch of science that involves studying how different substances react to each other

Declaration of Independence A document adopted on 4 July 1776 declaring that the colonies of America were no longer part of the British Empire but formed into the United States of America

gold panning A method of searching for gold dust that involves scooping up dirt and other material in a pan, then shaking the pan in water

joss house An informal name for a Chinese temple

Magna Carta First issued in the year 1215, this document aimed to limit the powers of the king and give more rights to others

malleable Able to be shaped by hammering or pressing

miner A person whose job involves digging underground in search of valuable substances, such as gold

quartz A very shiny crystal that is found in many kinds of roc

squatters People who live in a place that they do not own, without permission

tax An amount of money that people are required to pay t the government to help pay for the roads, schools, and other buildings and systems needed by the community

vault A secure room in which valuable items, such as gold bars, are kept